GREAT ILLUSTRATED CLASSICS

CAPTAINS COURAGEOUS

Rudyard Kipling

adapted by
Malvina Vogel

Illustrations by
Ken Landgraf

BARONET BOOKS, New York, New York

26958

Contents

About the Author

Rudyard Kipling was born in 1865, in Bombay, India, to English parents. Because he was cared for by Indian nurses for six years, he spoke Hindustani and was filled with Indian folk tales. These tales provided him with settings and background material for many of his poems and stories, including "Gunga Din," *Kim, Soldiers Three,* and *The Jungle Books.*

Although he grew up in England, Kipling returned to India at the age of seventeen to write for a newspaper. After seven years, a job offer as a reporter on a London newspaper brought him back to England. Shortly after that, Kipling moved to the United States, where he married an American woman and settled in Vermont.

His life in New England provided the background for one of his most famous novels for children — *Captains Courageous,* published in 1897. Since Kipling had spent years as a reporter, he was accustomed to collecting facts, and the novel is filled with details of fishing operations and the sea. But Kipling also excelled at characterizations, and in this novel, he was intent on picturing two courageous captains: the traditional New England fishing boat captain, who went to sea with his son at his side, and the captain of industry, who was building an empire for himself and his son.

Even though his political opinions caused him to lose popularity in later years, Kipling received the Nobel Prize for Literature in 1907, and continued writing until his death, in 1936.

The Liner's Dangerous Speed!

CHAPTER 1

Boy Overboard!

The North Atlantic fog rolled over the huge ocean liner and over the schooners and dories of a fishing fleet. It was May and the cod were running off Newfoundland, in the area known as the Grand Banks.

The liner's foghorn sounded its mournful warning with regularity, but the huge ship did not slow its speed, despite the fact that the speed was dangerous for the small boats that couldn't maneuver out of the way of the liner's cutting prow and powerful engine screw.

The thick fog crept into the liner's smoking room through an open door. A man reading a newspaper shivered, then got up and shut the door with a bang.

"That Cheyne boy is the biggest nuisance aboard," he complained to the other readers. "He leaves the door open just to irritate people."

A white-haired German nodded in agreement. "Spoiled, like many rich Americans."

Another man looked up from his book. "*Rich* is an understatement for the Cheynes," he said. "The old man owns half a dozen railroads, most of the lumber on the Pacific coast, and countless mines, just to start the list."

The man who had closed the door said, "Just the same, it's ridiculous for him to give his son two hundred dollars a month in allowance, even if he is an only child. And I'll bet he can worm twice that amount out of his mother when he wants to. She can't manage him, but he can certainly manage *her*."

The newspaper reader gave a short laugh.

Shutting Out the Fog

"She told me she's taking him to Europe to finish his education. Soon he'll be the most traveled know-nothing around. His best subjects will still be arrogance and rudeness! And it's a pity, because there's a lot of good in the boy if someone could only get through to him."

All the men looked up as the door to the smoking room was flung open. A boy of about fifteen entered. He was thin and slightly built, with a pasty yellow complexion. Ashes from his cigarette fell onto his red jacket, which matched the cap he wore pushed back on his light, curly hair. He sauntered into the room and perched on a table, knocking some magazines onto the floor.

The man who had shut the door before called loudly, "Close the door and stay outside, Harvey. You're not wanted here."

Harvey Cheyne tilted his chin up impudently. "Do you plan to throw me out, Mr. Martin? You didn't pay my way. This room is

Harvey Flings the Door Open.

open to all passengers. And if you want the door shut, shut it yourself!"

With a muttered oath, Mr. Martin slammed the door and returned to his paper. The other men ignored Harvey.

Determined to be noticed, Harvey said loudly, "Say, the fog is real thick. You can hear the fishing boats ringing their bells when we get close. Wouldn't it be great if we ran one down in the fog?"

The man with the book turned a page and made no reply. Nor did any of the others.

Harvey frowned and ground out the remains of his cigarette on the floor. Making one more bid for attention, he took a roll of bills from his pocket and began to count them. "How about a little poker?" he asked, glancing about. "I don't care how high the stakes."

Getting only silence as a reply, Harvey put away his money and turned his attention to the books lining one wall of the room. "Those books are all junk," he said with contempt.

"How About a Little Poker?"

"We have a better library in my father's hunting lodge in the Adirondacks. Ours are all bound in blue leather with real gold lettering."

This was too much for the man reading a book. "What's the binding got to do with the contents of a book?" he snapped.

Harvey shrugged, glad at last to be spoken to. "My mother always likes the book bindings to match the color scheme in each room."

"Heard your mother's been seasick. Too bad," observed the man more gently.

"Yes," said Harvey, "but she always gets sick on the ocean. Now I haven't been sick at all, except for a tiny bit the first day." He looked around for approval and saw the German looking at him shrewdly. Boldly, Harvey said to him, "Got a cigarette? I can't bear that mild junk the steward sells. I prefer Turkish tobacco every time."

In reply, the German opened his cigar case and held it out. Harvey strolled over and hesitated a moment before accepting one of

Offering Harvey a Cigar

the long, skinny black cigars.

"Dot is a man's smoke," said the German as Harvey lit the cigar with a flourish, confident that he was being accepted in grown-up society. "You like it?"

Harvey was so intent on drawing in the smoke that he didn't notice the smiles of the other men in the room. He inhaled deeply. "Oh, yes, very good flavor," he said, trying to give the impression that he was accustomed to such cigars, though it was his first.

But soon, his eyes filled with tears from the harsh smoke, and his stomach began to heave. He stood by the table, swaying a bit. "I think I'll go outside for a moment and see how the fog is doing," he said weakly. And as quickly as he was able, he staggered from the smoking room.

The men laughed loudly and returned to their reading.

Harvey staggered over the wet deck to the nearest rail. Nearby, a steward was lashing

Harvey's Stomach Begins to Ache.

deck chairs together. Because Harvey had bragged to everyone that he was never seasick and refused to be seen in such a condition, he forced himself to continue down to the second deck, well out of sight. In a very shaky state, he crawled to the deserted stern of the ship by the flagpole. There, as the big waves were leaping up, along with his stomach, Harvey doubled up in agony. His head swelled, sparks danced before his eyes, and weakness closed in on his whole body. Because he was close to fainting, he couldn't grip the rail too firmly.

The ship dipped down as a towering wave rose up. The dipping pulled the limp Harvey over the rail and into the green depths of the sea. The water closed over him, and Harvey blacked out.

Overboard!

Dead or Alive?

CHAPTER 2

Manuel's Big Fish

Harvey was awakened by a horn blowing in his ear. It sounded like the dinner-horn of a summer camp he had once attended. Was he back there? No, now he remembered. He was dead, drowned by the sea. That's why he felt so tired. But what was that strange smell all around him? It made him gag, and he brought up some of the salt water in him.

As he opened his eyes, he saw the sea all around him, and himself lying on a silver mound of half-dead fish. In front of him was the broad back of a man in a blue jersey. What with the salt water in him and the fish underneath him, Harvey felt sick again. He groaned.

The blue jersey turned around, showing a pair of gold earrings half-hidden in curly black hair. "Aha," said the man with a laugh, "my big fish wakes up. You better now?"

Harvey looked around. He realized that he was in a small boat, with the rough ocean so close that he shuddered with fear. But he also realized that he was alive. "Where am I?" he gasped.

"You are with Manuel, in dory. I see you fall out. Same time your big boat almost hit me. You go down, and I think you cut into bait by the screw. But you come up, and drift, drift to me. So I catch you."

Between every few words, Manuel lifted a conch shell to his lips and sent a boneshattering shriek through the fog.

Harvey could not move from the mound of fish, for there was no place in the flat-bottomed boat not covered by them. But he did shut his eyes against the mountainous

In Manuel's Dory

waves that dipped the dory up and down, twenty feet at a time.

Soon he imagined he heard the sound of a gun and another horn and some shouting. Then he felt himself, boat and all, being lifted in the air, then dropped into a dark hole. Peering through half-closed eyes, he saw two men in oilskins coming at him. They stripped off his wet clothes and forced a hot drink down him. Exhausted, Harvey fell into a deep sleep.

When Harvey woke up, he expected to hear the breakfast bell on the liner. Looking around, he wondered why his stateroom had grown so small. Then his eyes focused on a smiling, sunburned boy, about his own age, sitting on a table that Harvey could touch from his bunk. Behind the boy were other bunks, with black and yellow oilskins hanging and swaying beside them. Their strong smell mixed with the cabin's other smells: fried fish, burnt grease, paint, and stale tobacco. Harvey saw with disgust that his bunk had no sheets

Waking in a Strange Stateroom

but only dingy, lumpy ticking.

"Feeling better?" asked the boy. "Have some coffee." He filled a tin cup and put in molasses to sweeten the brew.

"Isn't there milk for it?" demanded Harvey.

"Well, no," said the boy in surprise. "And there won't be any till mid-September, when we get back to port. But the coffee's okay. I made it myself."

Harvey drank in silence, then ravenously ate a plateful of crisp fried pork.

"I'm Dan Troop," said the boy, "and my father's captain of the *We're Here*. I'm the cook's helper and do everything the other men won't do," he added proudly.

When Harvey finished eating, Dan made him stretch in every direction to find if he had any injuries. Satisfied that there were none, he handed him his clothes, which by now were dry. "And hurry up!" said Dan. "Dad's waiting for you.'"

Harvey looked at this crude but kind boy

Dan Gives Harvey His Dry Clothes.

with some amazement, unaccustomed as he was to being given orders by anyone. Then he arrogantly replied, "If your dad's so anxious to see me, he can come down here."

Dan's blue eyes opened wide. With a big grin at the boy's joke, he shouted Harvey's answer up the hatch.

The response came down from the deck in the deepest voice Harvey had ever heard. "Quit fooling, Dan, and send him to me."

Hurriedly, Dan scrambled among the high rubber boots strewn around the cabin and threw Harvey his once-white boating shoes.

Realizing the firmness of the voice on deck and believing that a few words from him to the captain would reveal his identity and get the boat turned around to New York, Harvey put on the shoes and hoisted himself up the ladder and out onto the deck.

Looking about him, he saw the *We're Here* riding anchor in an oily sea. On the horizon were other sailing vessels, and between them

Dan Shouts His Answer Up the Hatch.

in the water were dories out fishing.

Harvey made his way aft, stumbling over fishing gear on the deserted deck, to a small, thick-set, clean-shaven man sitting on the step that led to the quarter-deck. His blue eyes were the mirror of Dan's, but wiser and deeper.

"Morning—no, good afternoon, I should say. You near slept around the clock, young feller," said Captain Disko Troop, Dan's father. "Well, let's hear how it happened."

This greeting of "young feller" annoyed Harvey. Besides, he had almost drowned, and this man didn't even offer sympathy for all of his suffering. But Harvey answered in detail, ending with the demand, "You are to take me to New York immediately, and my father will pay you anything you ask."

"Hmm," said the man. "I don't think much of any man or boy who falls off one of them liners in a flat, calm sea. Especially with the excuse of being seasick."

"Excuse!" cried Harvey. "Do you imagine

"Take Me to New York Immediately!"

I'd fall overboard into your dirty boat for the fun of it — me, the son of Harvey Cheyne, Sr.!"

"Not knowing your idea of fun, or even who Harvey Cheyne, Sr., is, I can't say," said Disko. "But I do know it annoys my feelings to hear Manuel's boat called names. But speaking of names, I'm Disko Troop, and you're on my boat, the *We're Here,* out of Gloucester."

"I don't care who you are!" shrieked Harvey. "I'm grateful to you for saving me, but I must insist that you start for New York this minute."

Then remembering the money he had been counting in the smoking room, Harvey reached into his pocket. "I'll even give you an advance on the reward," he said grandly. But his hand came up empty. "I've been robbed! A hundred and thirty dollars! Give it back!"

Troop let the accusation pass, then raised a quizzical gray eyebrow. "And what's a young

"I've Been Robbed!"

feller like you doing with a sum of money like that?"

"It was part of my monthly allowance," said Harvey, thinking that would really impress the man.

Troop studied the boy thoughtfully for several minutes, then asked, "Do you remember hitting your head when you fell? I remember one sailor who tripped on a hatch and butted his head agin the mainmast. When he come to, he declared war on the British. They put him in a straight jacket for the rest of the trip. Now he's home, playing with rag dolls."

Though Harvey kept up his wild accusations about having been robbed, Disko didn't get angry. "Now, look here, young feller," he said. "We've just come a thousand miles to the Banks to fish. It's our living. With luck, we'll return to shore in September."

"But this is May!" cried Harvey. "I can't stay here and do nothing while you fish."

"Do You Remember Hitting Your Head?"

"Then here's what I'll do," said Disko. "You can help Dan for the trip. Ten and a half dollars a month and a share in the profits, same as the rest of us."

"Do you mean I'm to clean pots and things?" screamed Harvey, almost dancing with rage.

Troop nodded calmly. "And you've no cause to shout."

"I won't!" cried Harvey, stomping on the deck. "I won't do your filthy scrubbing on this fish kettle. I tell you my father will buy you ten boats like this if you take me to New York now. And you can keep the hundred and thirty dollars."

At that point, Dan took Harvey's arm. "Don't go on like this with Dad. He don't take being called a thief by any man."

"I won't stop!" cried Harvey, pulling his arm away.

Troop sat staring at the mast as Harvey continued his ranting. Finally, he spoke. "I

"I Won't Do Your Filthy Scrubbing!"

don't blame you none, young feller. You're not yourself. But my offer of second cabin boy holds. How about it?"

"No!" screamed Harvey with all his might. "Take me back or—"

Harvey didn't remember what happened next, but a minute later he found himself on the deck with blood streaming from his nose.

Disko Troop motioned Dan over. "Son," he said solemnly, "never be led astray by hasty judgments like just happened to me. I was set agin this boy when I first saw him. Now I'm plumb sorry for him. He's clear distracted in his head. He ain't responsible for all he's been saying to me. Now you treat him gentle. The bleeding will help clear his head. And remember what I say about hasty judgments." Then he went below.

"The Bleeding Will Help Clear His Head."

"I Tried To Warn You."

CHAPTER 3

Harvey Lends a Hand

Dan sat on the coiled rope and shook his head in sympathy. "I tried to warn you."

Harvey's tears of rags and pain mingled with the blood from his nose. "That man's crazy," he moaned, "and I'm helpless."

"Now that's a funny turnaround," replied Dan. "He thinks *you're* the crazy one, with your wild yarns about your piles of money. Come on below and get washed off."

Grateful to Dan, Harvey poured out more of the "wild yarn" of his background. Dan's eyes opened wide at the tale of houses, servants, mines, businesses, and railroads, including two private cars, the *Constance,* named after Harvey's mother, and the *Harvey.*

Finally Dan said, "Will you swear on all this? Will you say, 'Hope I may die if I ain't speaking truth'?"

"I swear," said Harvey solemnly.

Dan was a younger edition of his father and accustomed to making up his own mind. Slowly, a grin spread over his face. "I believe you're speaking truth, Harvey, most of it, anyway. I guess Dad's made a mistake, thinking you're crazy. He put a lot of store by his good judgment, so there'll be a real gale when he has to admit he's wrong. But he's a just man, who don't show no favorites, not even to me, his son, when it comes to work or money — which we don't have much of."

Harvey's nose had stopped bleeding and he had washed his face. He smiled back at Dan, grateful that he had found an ally. "So I was right — he did take my money."

Dan held up a weather-beaten hand. "Now

Harvey Swears That His Story Is True.

hold on there. You were wrong! Dad'll just fetch you another wallop if you go on like that. No one on the *We're Here* is a thief. We're fishermen. I can't say what happened to your money. I didn't even look in your pockets when I dried out your clothes."

This reminder of his rescue made Harvey pause. After a few moments he said slowly, "I guess I haven't been very grateful to you. I could be dead now instead of here, and I *could* have lost my money."

"Well, you been shook up by all this," said Dan. "I guess I can understand."

Harvey drew a deep breath. "I want to see your father. Please take me to his cabin."

Dan led Harvey to Disco Troop's cabin, where they found the captain making entries in a notebook.

Meekly, Harvey spoke. "I haven't acted quite right, sir, and I'm here to apologize. When a man is saved from drowning, he shouldn't start calling people names right

Harvey Apologizes to Disko.

away. So I'm here to say I'm sorry." He waited timidly for Troop's reply.

Troop heaved himself off the locker he was sitting on and held out his large hand. " I knew a little blood-letting would clear your head. I'm seldom wrong about my judgments." And he shook Harvey's hand heartily, numbing the boy's arm to the elbow. But Harvey didn't wince as Troop went on. "Now, young feller, you go along with Dan and do as he does. We'll work you hard, but fair. And maybe you'll get some muscle in those stringy arms."

Harvey felt an unaccustomed pride as he and Dan went back on deck. Dan was insistent on also shaking his hand. "Dad's right, you know," he said. "We couldn't take you back now. Fishing's our living, and we're just starting to fill her up." He pointed to the open main-hatch between the two masts.

As Harvey peered into the large, empty space, Dan said, "We got to fill her with cod, all salted down."

A Hearty Handshake!

"And where are the fish?" asked Harvey.

Dan laughed. "There's a saying about the fish," he explained. "It goes, 'In the sea they say; in the boats we pray.' Manuel brought you in with about forty cod that are waiting in the pen to be split and cleaned."

By now the sun was sinking, changing the green water to purple and pink with golden lights. The dories were heading to their schooners, looking like tiny toy boats in the distance.

Pointing to one, Dan said, "There's Manuel. He ain't got room for another fish. See how low he is in the water, just like a lily-pad."

"He's a foreigner, isn't he?"

"Yes, Portuguese. And Long Jack's from Ireland, but lives in Boston. The rest—" Dan broke off as a melodious song reached them over the sea.

Dan chuckled and explained, "That's Tom Platt. He always sings when he's got a full boat."

The Dories Return to Their Schooners.

A few minutes later, Manuel's dory drew alongside. With a short-handled fork, he began to toss his fish up into a wooden pen on deck. "Two hundred and thirty-one," he shouted up to the boys as he finished.

"We got to hoist him in now," Dan told Harvey. "Take a-hold of that tackle behind you."

Harvey grabbed at a rope and long iron hook dangling from one of the stays of the mainmast as Dan seized another.

"Give him the hook," ordered Dan.

Harvey let the hook down into Manuel's hands. The fisherman slipped it through a loop of rope at the bow of his dory, then did the same with Dan's hook at the stern.

Climbing aboard the *We're Here,* Manuel gave Harvey a huge grin, but Harvey had no time to smile back for Dan was shouting, "Pull!"

Harvey pulled and was astonished to find how easily the dory rose.

Manuel Tosses His Fish Up onto the Deck.

"Lower away!" ordered Dan when the boat was above their heads.

Harvey and Dan lowered, and Dan swayed the dory with one hand until it landed lightly just behind the mainmast. He nodded approvingly at Harvey. "A dory don't weigh nothing when it's empty, but that was right good for a passenger."

Harvey turned to Manuel, who regarded him through snapping black eyes. "So, you are well now," said the fisherman with a laugh. "Last night the fish fish for you. Tonight you fish for them."

"I'm . . . I'm ever so grateful to you," stammered Harvey, feeling shy in front of his benefactor. His hand automatically went to his back pocket to reward Manuel before he remembered he did not have any money. When he knew Manuel better, the thought of the mistake he might have made if he had offered money to such a man would have made him squirm with embarrassment. Instead, he held

Hoisting the Dory On Board

out his hand to offer his thanks.

Manuel took the boy's hand in his strong, tanned ones, saying, "No need to be grateful. What else should I do? Let you drift all around the Banks?" Then he started bending forward and back from the hips to get out the kinks from hours spent in the dory.

"Danny, my boy," he said, straightening up, "I have not cleaned my boat today. The fish struck too quick. You do it for me, yes?"

Harvey stepped forward at once. Here was something he could do for the man who had saved his life. "Please let me do it, Manuel." And he picked up a swab, leaned over the dory, and began mopping up the slime, clumsily but eagerly.

Meanwhile, Tom Platt's catch was pouring into the pen on top of Manuel's. Dan and Manuel swung Platt's dory aboard and nested it inside Manuel's.

The other dories followed close after. Harvey, not knowing what else to do as the

Harvey Eagerly Swabs Manuel's Dory.

men helped Dan swing the dories in, started swabbing out each one as it nested down.

Dan called out introductions between Harvey and the incoming men. They nodded to him agreeably, especially as they noticed his energy and enthusiasm at swabbing in spite of his inexperience.

At the cook's call, most of the men went below to eat. Dan, however, motioned to Harvey to wait, then led him into the hold, where he showed him how to knock open the barrels of salt.

A second call of "Seat ye! Seat ye!" came in a while. It was Harvey's turn to eat, along with Dan, Manuel, and Penn, the youngest fisherman. Penn asked a blessing over the cod, pork, and fried potatoes. In a moment the cook, a huge, dark Negro, had added hot bread and coffee to the table. He did not talk, but smiled at Harvey's appetite.

The day's work was still not ended for the crew of the *We're Here.* They took up positions

Penn Asks a Blessing Over the Food.

around the wooden pen and around a table, and down in the hold. The first man seized a cod, slit it open, and passed it on. The second man scooped out the cod's liver into a basket, then flung the rest of its innards and head onto the deck. The empty fish was passed next on to a man who ripped out its backbone. Then it was flung into a tub of salt water.

When the tub was full, Harvey was given the order, "Pitch!" And Dan showed him how to pitch the cod down the hatch by twos and threes.

In the hold, salt was rubbed on the fish, and they were packed tightly together, now preserved for the long months before they reached the market.

At the end of an hour, Harvey would have given anything to rest. The fresh, wet cod weighed more than he thought possible, and his back ached from pitching. Yet he held on stubbornly, proud that for the first time in his life he was part of a working gang of men.

Pitching the Cod Down the Hatch

At intervals, Dan sent him to collect the dulled knives and to supply sharp ones. Another change came when Dan's Uncle Salters called, "Knife oh!" and everyone stopped work to stretch and try to get rid of kinks. At these points, Harvey was sent for water. He passed around dipperfuls of stale brown water, which, in these circumstances, tasted delicious.

Finally, the last cod was gutted and salted down, and the exhausted men turned in to sleep immediately. But Dan and Harvey had to wash the pen and table. Then while Dan sharpened the knives on a tiny grindstone, Harvey swept fish bones and innards off the deck and into the water.

At the first splash, a silvery-white ghost bolted up from the oily water with a weird, whistling sigh. Harvey jumped back from the rail with a shout.

"It's only a grampus," said Dan, laughing. "They beg for fishheads. They up-end like that

Sharpening Knives and Sweeping the Deck

when they're hungry. You'll see hundreds of 'em 'fore you're through. Now we have to take the first watch."

Harvey was ready to fall in his tracks, but Dan warned him that he would keep him awake with a sharp blow from a knotted rope whenever he nodded off to sleep.

"But look how calm it is," argued Harvey. "And the moon makes it bright as day. What's to hurt us?"

"Dad has always warned me that it's just on nights like tonight that a liner could bear down and cut our schooner in two because we're not expecting any trouble."

Still, despite Dan's chattering, Harvey dozed off several times, only to be awakened by a blow from Dan's rope and a scolding.

But at last, the cabin clock struck ten, and Penn crept on deck. As soon as he appeared, both Harvey and Dan fell down where they stood, fast asleep. Another day on the *We're Here* had finally ended.

Dan Wakes Harvey with a Rope.

Helping the Cook

CHAPTER 4

Flight into the Fog

The next day dawned mild and clear. After a big breakfast, Harvey worked willingly with Dan at their chores. They washed the plates and pots from the crew's meal, then helped send the fishermen out in their dories. They sliced pork for the midday meal and carried coal and water into the cook. As they filled the lamps and swabbed the deck, Dan talked and Harvey listened, eager to know everything about his new life.

"One thing I got to warn you about is Penn," said Dan. "I mean, not exactly him, but about reminding him who he really is."

Harvey's eyes brightened at a mystery. "Who is he? He's not nearly as big and strong as the rest of the men."

"That's because he's really a preacher. Or was, I should say. Right now, Penn ain't himself, but he's nowise dangerous."

"Oh?" said Harvey rather sharply. "Is that really so, or is it another of your father's famous judgments?"

Dan rested on his mop for a moment. "No, it's the truth. Dad told me that Penn had a wife and four children back in Pennsylvania, where he did preaching. One day, they went to Johnstown for a church meeting. First thing you know, the Johnstown flood happened. Near wiped out the whole town. Uncle Salters, my dad's brother, then took care of Penn on his farm ever since the accident."

"Why, I've heard of that flood," said Harvey excitedly. "A dam burst."

"That's right," said Dan. "The flood swept away Penn's family right before his eyes. He

66

The Flood Swept Away Penn's Family.

got saved somehow, but his mind cracked from losing his wife and kids like that. He wandered off, and Uncle Salters kinda found him, but he don't remember any of that life."

"I'll be careful not to remind him," said Harvey. "But how come he's here and not on your uncle's farm?"

Harvey finished his section of the deck before replying. "Penn's church finally traced him and wanted him to come home. But Uncle Salters was agin it. He says if Penn ever remembers who he is and what happened, he'll just up and die. So Uncle Salters sold the farm, and him and Penn signed on the *We're Here* to fish. The church wouldn't think of hunting for Penn on the Banks."

As they swabbed the deck, Dan kept an eye on his father, who sat smoking near his cabin and watching an increasing number of schooners surround the *We're Here*. It was well known that Disko Troop could smell out the best fishing grounds around, so other

Signing On the *We're Here*

boats followed him closely. While Troop appreciated this tribute to his powers, it did not suit his pocket.

Yesterday's fishing had brought fewer and smaller cod than the previous catch, and he predicted the same for today's. Drawing deeply on his pipe, he tried to take the viewpoint of a twenty-pound cod and decide where the big fish would have gone, considering the recent gales, currents, and its favorite food. After an hour of almost trance-like thought, Disko Troop rose, took the pipe from his teeth, and nodded his head confidently.

When Dan saw this, he judged it was safe to approach his father. "Dad, we've done our chores. Can we take my dory out for a spot of fishing?"

"You're free to go, Danny." Whenever he called his son "Danny," it was a sign that he was pleased with life. "But get Harvey into some decent rig," he added. "I never saw

Unwelcome Company

anything so terrible as that red jacket and white shoes of his."

Delighted, Dan dragged Harvey down into the cabin and began rummaging through a locker. Soon Harvey was outfitted in a heavy blue jersey, clean but patched, an oilskin hat and slicker, and a pair of rubber boots that came halfway up his thighs.

"Now you look a fisherman," said Dan with a smile.

The boys lowered Dan's little red dory, the *Hattie S.* Dan jumped in lightly and frowned at the clumsy way Harvey tumbled in after him. "That's no way to get in a boat," he said. "You got to learn to meet her as she comes up."

Harvey accepted the criticism because it was obvious he was far from imitating Dan's easy drop. Next, Harvey's rowing drew Dan's exasperation. "Short! Row short!" he ordered. "Else the sea'll just whip your oar around if she rises. You're not on an Adirondack pond,

Dan Outfits Harvey in Fisherman's Clothes.

you know. This dory's all mine. Ain't she a daisy?"

Harvey spoke between gasps as he tried to pull short strokes with his oar. "Yes, very nice. I might ask my father to get me one or two."

As if to pay him back for this smug comment, a sudden swell of the sea seized Harvey's oar and smacked the top of it under his chin with a hard crack.

"That's what I meant about rowing short," said Dan. "I had to learn too, but I was eight years old when that happened to me last."

As Harvey got back into position, frowning and rubbing his jaw, Dan went on. "No good getting mad at things like that. Dad says it's our own fault if we can't handle 'em."

Dan didn't anchor the dory, but let it drift until he could estimate the best spot to fish. He showed Harvey how to bait his hook with a salt clam and then feed down the line without snarling it. By the time Harvey managed

A Crack on the Chin from an Oar

to get his line ready, Dan was already pulling in a cod. As it flapped alongside the dory, Dan called, "The muckle, Harvey, the muckle!"

Harvey had no idea what Dan wanted, but looked in the corner of the boat where Dan was pointing. He decided that the large wooden hammer was what Dan wanted and quickly handed it over. Dan grabbed it and stunned the cod with a blow. Then he hauled it in and removed the hook.

At that moment, Harvey felt a tug on his own hook. He pulled the line up easily. "Why, these are bunches of strawberries!" he cried.

"Don't touch 'em!" shouted Dan, but Harvey had already pulled them from his hook to admire them. They were perfect reproductions of the land fruit except there were no leaves, the stems were scaly and slimy, and the fruit was covered with sharp, pointed spines.

Dan's warning had come too late. Harvey's hand had already been stung by the straw-

"The Muckle, Harvey, the Muckle!"

berries' needle-like spines. "Ouch!" he cried, and flung them back into the sea.

"Now you know what a strawberry-bottom is," said Dan.

Harvey smiled, then baited up again, having learned another lesson of the sea. The instant he let down his hook, the line flashed through his hands. "What is it?" he cried. "It feels like I've caught a whale!"

Dan peered into the water, where something large and white flicked. "Halibut, I think. Looks about a hundred pounds. Let me help you."

"No, you won't!" shouted Harvey. "It's my first fish, and I'll get him alone."

His knuckles banged against the side of the boat and began to bleed, but he held on. Sweat streamed from his face, which was almost purple from exertion. For the next twenty minutes, the halibut circled and struggled. Dan stood ready with the muckle.

Then, just as Harvey reached the limit of his

Stung by the Strawberries

endurance, the fish gave in. It flopped alongside, Dan whacked it, and Harvey heaved it
into the dory. Harvey could hardly believe he
had caught such a huge, gray monster. Though
every inch of him ached, he had never been
happier or prouder!

At that moment, a pistol shot cracked
through the air, and a potato basket was run
up in the front rigging of the *We're Here*.

"What's it mean?" asked Harvey.

"Dad wants everyone back on board. He's
got some plan, or else he'd never break off
fishing this time of day."

The crew responded quickly to Disko
Troop's summons. At first he only said to
them, "We'll start the dressing down now. Get
out the table and knives, Danny."

But as they started cutting and salting the
catch, Troop explained. "Boys, you can see for
yourselves on this table—there's no cod over
fifteen pounds. Harvey's halibut is the last big
fish we'll see in these parts. So we're moving

Proud of His Halibut

on, away from this crowd. Leave them to bait big and catch small."

Uncle Salters looked up from ripping out backbones. "When are we gettin' under way, Disko?"

"I'm waiting on the weather. Otherwise this crowd'll just tail along."

Harvey looked at the clear sky and wondered what the captain saw there. But a half-hour later, the Bank fog dropped on them. It curled and smoked along the colorless water, sealing each boat into itself. Without a command or a word to each other, the men stopped gutting cod and ran to heave up the anchor and raise the sail. With Disko Troop at the wheel, the *We're Here* silently stole away from the other fishing schooners and into the whirling fog.

The *We're Here* Silently Steals Away.

Penn and Uncle Salters Go Below.

CHAPTER 5

Disko Troop Proves Right

The *We're Here* made its way confidently through the fog, though Harvey could not see more than a few feet beyond the boat. "How can your father see where he's going?" he whispered to Dan.

"Dad don't need to see. He could sail the Banks blindfold." Dan stated this as a matter of fact and not in a bragging way.

Uncle Salters and Penn passed the boys on their way below.

"They're going to play checkers and drink coffee," Dan explained. "There's nothing so dead as a fishing boat that's not fishing."

Long Jack overheard this comment. "I'll give Harvey something to do. He can start in learning the ropes. Come on with me."

He led Harvey to one end of the boat and started naming every rope and piece of tackle, explaining the use of each one. Harvey was soon in a blur, mixing up a peak halyard with a reef-pennant. So when Long Jack asked him how to reef the foresail, he shook his head in ignorance.

"I see you need a little help to make you learn," said Long Jack. He picked up a length of rope and flicked it at Harvey, catching him sharply around the ribs. "Now we'll go around again with me learning ye. In between I'll ask my questions and this rope will tell you if you're wrong."

Harvey opened his mouth to protest such treatment, but then he saw Disko, Manuel, Dan, and the others staring at him. They didn't seem to think that Long Jack was being unfair, so Harvey clamped his mouth shut.

Long Jack Teaches Harvey About the Ropes.

Squaring his shoulders, he walked aft to where the lesson had begun before. He had more than average intelligence, but had always been too lazy to learn what didn't interest him, and no one had ever forced him to do so. This time, he concentrated and easily followed the logic of each rope's function in managing the sails.

At the end, when Long Jack questioned him, Harvey was able to answer correctly, even though it was not with the exact words. Long Jack only winced when Harvey said, "I'd let down the sail," but Manuel sang out, "*Lower* the sail. Later, I show you a little schooner I make with all her ropes. Then you get all names very fixed in your mind."

At Disko Troop's call, Tom Platt started measuring the depth of the sea by throwing out a line weighted at its end. As Tom hauled in wet coils of line, Dan asked his father, "What do you think the sounding will be, Dad?"

Harvey Learns Quickly.

Disko glanced at the compass, thought a moment, and said, "Sixty, maybe."

The next moment, Tom Platt sang out, "Sixty."

Dan turned to Harvey proudly. "See, he knows where we are and where the fish are; he can sail blindfold."

After another fifteen minutes, Disko again called, "Heave!"

This time, Tom Platt called, "Fifty."

"Let's bait up, Harve," called Dan, and they threw their lines over the side.

Within moments, a fish grabbed the bait on Dan's line, and Harvey helped him haul a twenty-pound cod onto the deck. Peering down at the fish, Harvey cried, "Why, he's all covered with little crabs! Is he still good to eat?"

"Sure," said Dan. "When they're lousy like that, it's a sign that they all been herding together by the thousand. And from the way he snapped up the bait, they're so hungry

Measuring Position and Depth

they'd bite on a bare hook."

With that, Harvey pulled up a crab-covered cod, as large as Dan's.

Tom Platt let out a cheer, crying, "Disko Troop, you got a pair of spare eyes hid under this boat to find the cod!"

The crew lowered the anchor and began fishing from the deck of the *We're Here*. The cod poured in, all of them crab-covered.

"This is great! " cried Harvey as he hauled in another large cod. "Why don't we fish from the boat all the time?"

"We can, until we start dressing down. Then, all them innards and heads we throw back in the sea scares the fish off. That's when we have to go out after them in the dories."

At last the cod stopped their eager biting, and the dressing down began. A call went out for Penn and Uncle Salters. Penn was too mild to complain, but Uncle Salters yelled in annoyance because no one had interrupted their game of checkers to say the cod were biting.

Harvey Pulls Up a Crab-Covered Cod.

Since a count was made of the number of cod each man took during the voyage, the more he caught, the more money he earned.

It also did not please Uncle Salters when Disko assigned him and Penn to do the cleanup of the cutting table and deck. But Disko pointed out that they had been idle while the others worked at catching cod.

Harvey and Dan were pleased to be rid of their nightly job, but Disko had another chore for them. "We're trawling tonight. Get cracking, Dan."

Dan groaned at his father's order, but he led Harvey to some large tubs containing coiled fishing lines. Big hooks were fastened to every few feet of line. The boys settled down to baiting the hooks and keeping the line untangled so it could be fed out easily.

Harvey sat over his tub and baited slowly. Partly he was awkward at it and partly he was trying — without much success — not to catch his fingers on the barbs. Dan's fingers flew,

Baiting the Hooks on the Trawl-Lines

like someone knitting.

"I helped bait up trawl on shore before I could even walk," he said, and Harvey felt better about his clumsiness and lack of speed.

When the trawl-lines were baited, Tom Platt and Long Jack heaved the tubs into a dory along with small buoys. With the dory riding very low in the water, they pushed off into the fog. Disko motioned Harvey over to a bell and told him to keep ringing it.

Harvey sent a clang, clang, clang into the fog to guide the two men back. When he peered into the mists, he could see nothing but the smoky air. But knowing that two men's lives depended on him, he kept up a steady ringing.

Relief flooded through Harvey when a hail through the fog announced the return of the trawl-layers.

Tom Platt gave Dan a friendly cuff on the shoulder as he came aboard, dripping. "Nary a snarl in that line," he said approvingly.

Guiding the Fishermen Back

The long, exciting day had so wearied Harvey that he fell asleep sitting at the table after dinner. Only his anxiety for the men's safety had kept him awake those hours, ringing the bell.

Penn looked down at the sleeping Harvey with sadness. Softly he said to Uncle Salters, "How sad his poor parents must be, for they think he's dead. How terrible it must be to lose a child — to lose a son!"

At this comment, Dan called in a loud, hearty voice, "Penn, go finish your checkers game with Uncle Salters."

Always agreeable, Penn joined Uncle Salters, forgetting about dead children and leaving Harvey — and soon Dan — in a sound, dreamless sleep.

Penn Is Sad for Harvey's Parents.

A Roller Coaster Ride at Sea!

CHAPTER 6

The Cook's Prophecy

Harvey woke the next morning on a roller coaster. Heavy seas sent the *We're Here* climbing up and up, then down and down, quivering all over. A pause. Then the seas crashed on the deck as the *We're Here* began to climb upward again. There could be no fishing in such a gale, but the trawl-lines were still out.

Harvey moved around slowly and carefully, wondering if he were going to be sick. Then he found he was wildly hungry, as always. He managed to eat his usual big breakfast, and saw he was not going to be sick. Then he and

Dan bustled around, doing chores for the cook. After having peeled potatoes, cut up pork, and brought up the coal, they were free.

Sitting in the cabin with the crew, with the gale still blowing, Harvey turned to Manuel and asked, " How long will it stay like this? "

"Maybe clear tonight, maybe two days more," he replied. "You not afraid?"

"No. I was just afraid of being sick," said Harvey. "But I feel fine."

"That is because we make fisherman of you. When we come back to Gloucester, you should burn two, three candles in our Church on the Hill, to the Virgin, for your luck. I do that," explained Manuel. "It is why very few Portuguese men ever drown."

Tom Platt shook his head. "I don't see it that way. The sea's the sea, and no candles are going to help."

Lighting his pipe, Long Jack added, "I'm with Manuel's way of thinking. It never hurt to have a friend at church."

Manuel's Advice

Dan did not join in the talk, but wrestled with an accordion and the pitching of the *We're Here*. He managed a recognizable playing of several popular sea chanteys, which the crew sang along with him. Then when he began another tune, Tom Platt roared out, "Hold on! That song's a Jonah for sure!"

"No, it's not," returned Dan hotly. "It's only a Jonah if you sing the last verse."

"What's a Jonah?" asked Harvey.

"Anything that spoils the luck," explained Long Jack. "Sometimes it's a person, or it could be a knife or even a bucket. There's all sorts of Jonahs."

Tom Platt said, "Jim Burke was one until he drowned last season. I'd rather have starved than ship out with Burke."

Dan joined in. "Remember the green dory on the *Ezra Flood?* That was the worst Jonah. Drowned four men, she did, and used to shine in the night."

"Is good Harvey is no Jonah," said Manuel.

Dan Entertains the Crew.

"It was a chance I took when I saved him."

"Of course he's not," said Dan hotly. "In fact, just the opposite. The day after he came on board, we had a toppin' good catch."

Suddenly, the cook gave a queer, thin laugh. He stopped peeling the potatoes in the large bowl in his lap and looked around at the men, ending with Harvey. "No, you are not a Jonah, but something else."

It was so unusual for the cook to speak that the men held very still and listened.

"In a few years, you will be Dan's master," he told Harvey. "And Dan will be your man."

"Not by a jugful," protested Dan. "Why do you say that?"

"I see it in my head. Harvey the master and Dan his man."

"Now how in thunder do you figure that?" said Tom Platt.

"I see it in my head," was the cook's only reply. "Harvey the master and Dan his man."

The Cook Makes a Prophecy.

Dan Clipped a Lock of Hattie's Hair.

CHAPTER 7

Harvey's "Friend"

Whether the days were fine or foggy, they all held new things for Harvey to learn. Some of them were personal, like Dan's entrusting him with his secret about the name *Hattie S.* on his dory. The real Hattie had sat in front of Dan last winter at school. Being fourteen, she had a contempt for all boys, but that had not stopped Dan from losing his heart to her. Swearing Harvey to secrecy, he had shown him his most precious possession — a lock of Hattie's hair. Sitting behind her, he had simply clipped it without her knowledge.

Another lesson was personal to Harvey. He

got boils between his elbows and wrists, where his wet jersey and oilskins cut into the flesh. Dan watched them with a professional eye. When he judged them ripe, he treated them with Disko's razor.

"Now you've been blooded," he told Harvey. "You're a real Banker. It's one of the things that happens to all of us."

Disko taught him to steer. Nothing thrilled Harvey more than feeling the ship respond to his hand. Without knowing it, he imitated Disko's peculiar stoop at the wheel, as if that were also part of steering correctly.

But pride in his new learning tripped him up once in a while. A combination of wind and forgetfulness about which sails were set brought Harvey a small wreckage — the stay-sail ripped right through. For the next few days, he spent his leisure time in mending the torn sail, under the instruction of Tom Platt. Harvey was awkward with the needle, but did a fair job for a beginner.

Disko Teaches Harvey to Steer.

This opinion was given to Long Jack by Platt, along with another one. "I wonder could Disko be wrong about the boy's madness? He strikes me sane as you."

Long Jack agreed and, over their evening meal, suggested to Disko that he must be mistaken about the boy.

Disko chewed for a while, then said, "Well, here's how I figure it. He was crazy as a loon when he come aboard. But I'll allow he's sobered up considerable since. So I must have cured him."

Harvey missed another chance to distinguish himself, but Long Jack saved the day. The *We're Here* met a French fishing boat, and waves and calls were exchanged.

"I'm plumb out of tobacco," complained Uncle Salters. "I bet they got plenty for sale."

When the rest of the crew announced a similar shortage, Disko agreed to send a dory over. "I ain't so sure you can make yourself understood," he told Long Jack.

Greeting a French Fishing Boat

"I speak French," piped up Harvey. *"Tabac* is the word for tobacco."

Long Jack turned to him excitedly. "Well then, Harvey, you come along to interpret."

Harvey was rushed to the rail with the crew surrounding him, and he bellowed, *"Attendez! Nous sommes venant pour tabac."*

The Frenchmen called back, "Ah, *tabac!"*

Long Jack and Harvey were quickly launched in a dory and hauled up on the foreign boat. There, Harvey stated the quantity of tobacco needed and asked the price. Silence met his efforts. He went through his request again.

One of the Frenchmen stepped forward and answered, but Harvey had no idea what he was saying. And beyond the one word *tabac,* they didn't understand Harvey.

When Long Jack realized that Harvey didn't speak or understand the French used by these men who fished the Banks, he waded in with gestures and arm waving. The French

Long Jack Takes Over.

crew responded in a like manner, and soon a trade was arranged. Harvey was then sent back for cocoa tins and bags of crackers.

A swap was made, and he and Long Jack returned to the *We're Here* with numerous cakes of chewing and smoking tobacco. After that, the men would often tease Harvey by shouting *"Tabac"* at him, but he took it good-naturedly.

The truth of the matter is that Harvey even welcomed the teasing. It meant that he belonged, that he was considered one of the crew *by* the crew. At times, when he thought about his mother, it was with impatience, for he was keen to tell her about his new life. He wanted her to know that he was accepted by these fine fishermen.

Harvey's acceptance by the crew was most evident in the long conversations they had together when storms kept them idle. Manuel talked about pretty girls. Long Jack held them spellbound with tales of the supernatural. And

Returning to the *We're Here* with Tobacco

Disko told of great whale hunts. Harvey's contributions to the conversations — descriptions of his life before the *We're Here* — began to be much appreciated because they were so foreign to the men. But since he was afraid of a wallop from Disko if he claimed the experiences for himself, he invented a "friend."

Harvey told of a friend who ordered five suits of clothes at a time, drove a coach with four ponies, and went to parties where the guests brought presents made of silver. The crew goggled to hear about perfumes, small dinner parties, champagne, cigarettes with gold-leaf tips, jewelry, and big hotels.

Throughout it all, Dan and Harvey waited for the day when they could reveal who this "friend" really was.

Harvey's Tales of a "Friend"

Ordering Tom and Long Jack into the Dory

"Squid O!"

Having baited the trawl-lines once, Harvey understood why Dan had groaned when his father gave the order. It was boring work, and even Dan's able fingers had been stabbed by a hook or two. So when Disko said, "Tom Platt, Long Jack, time to see what we got on them lines," Harvey's spirits sank. Another long session over the bait tubs faced him and Dan. But to his surprise, Dan staggered from below with a tub and put it in Tom Platt's dory.

As the men launched the dory, Harvey asked Dan, "Don't we have to bait?"

"No, they do it. They take a cod off the hook

and put a piece of bait back on," replied Dan "It's just like taking clothes off a washline and putting others up, using the same clothes-pins."

"It might be said to be like that," said his father, overhearing his explanation. "But I've seen that long, sagging line twitch a boat under in a flash. And the more you load your dory, the more you got to watch out."

By now the dory was out of sight, and Harvey was sent to the bell, for a fog had closed in. Tom Platt and Long Jack were gone such a long time that Harvey began to fear for them. But then through the swirling mists, a sound came over the water.

"And now to thee, O Captain," sang a familiar voice. The dory was alongside the *We're Here,* well-loaded, with Tom Platt singing at the top of his voice. And he didn't stop, but serenaded Long Jack as he forked the cod into the pen on board.

"Disko, send down another tub of bait,"

Taking Off Cod and Putting On Bait

called Long Jack when all the fish were aboard. "They was biting almost before we got the hooks back in the water. "

Harvey lugged up the tub this time, and the dory pushed off into the fog once more. Returning to the bell again, Harvey resumed his ringing, confident now that it would guide the two men home safely and that they were masters of the trawl.

The bait tub that Harvey had passed down into the dory contained clams, but the best cod-bait was found the next night. The ship was on the eastern edge of the Grand Banks in forty fathoms of water. Uncle Salters was on watch. In the middle of the night, he gave a yell that woke everyone aboard.

"Squid O!" bellowed Uncle Salters.

Harvey hurried on deck with the rest, and Dan gave him a squid-jig — a piece of lead, painted red. There was a circle of pins at the lower end bent backward like half-opened umbrella ribs.

"Squid O!"

"Do I put the bait on the pins?" Harvey asked.

"No," said Dan. "That's all you need right there. For some reason — even Dad don't know why — the squid likes the rig. He wraps himself around it, and you haul him up before he can escape from the pins."

Harvey dropped his jig over the side and in a moment, felt an extra weight and a tug. He hauled in quickly, but as the squid got clear of the water, it sent a stream of water into Harvey's face. Harvey kept hauling, but before he could detach the squid from the rig, it squirted ink into his eyes.

"Oh, oh!" cried Harvey, dropping the rig and the squid and wiping out his eyes.

Dan looked over as ink splashed on the side of his hair. "You got to dodge, Harv. They'll get you in the face every time if you don't."

As he looked about him, Harvey saw the men darting their heads from side to side as they hauled in. But they could not keep the

The Squid Squirts Ink.

ink from landing somewhere on them. Harvey was caught several more times full in the face with ink, and everyone was black with it by the time the run ended.

Disko was pleased. "Nothing a cod likes better than a little shiny piece of squid tentacle at the tip of a clam-baited hook."

Harvey didn't say so aloud, but he thought the cod very sensible for letting others get a face full of ink while *it* got a tasty morsel.

Black with Squid Ink

Taking Turns on the Bell

CHAPTER 9

Penn Remembers — and Forgets

As the *We're Here* worked her way northward, she was joined by others fishing the same waters. When a heavy fog rolled in, Disko suspended work and anchored. Harvey and Dan took turns on the bell, for Disko was always afraid of being run down by a liner. The sound of the bell was thin and forlorn, pinched off by the thick, foggy air.

Suddenly, in the distance, the muffled shriek of a liner's siren reached Harvey's ears. Fearful, he tried to sound the bell harder, but without success. Suddenly, he remembered a smoking room, where a boy in a red jacket was trying to draw attention to himself. The boy was saying, "Wouldn't it be great if we ran one down in the fog?" *One* meant a fishing boat . . . like the very one he was on right now. He also remembered the thirty-foot steel prow of the liner, storming through the waves at twenty miles an hour. If she caught the *We're Here* in her path, she would grind the small schooner right through. How he despised that boy in the red jacket for his silly, dangerous talk!

There was a stirring in the air. From his post at the rail, Harvey felt himself near a moving body. For a moment, his hand faltered on the bell, then rang it madly. For the wet edge of an immense bow was bearing down on the schooner, a feather of foamy water curling in front of it. A swell of the sea pushed the *We're Here* slightly to one side, and a line of brass-rimmed portholes flashed past. The danger came and went before Harvey had time to cry out or faint or be sick. He held onto the rail tightly as the wake of the liner rocked the

Brassed-Rimmed Portholes Flash Past.

schooner like a cradle. Then, through the fog, came a crack, and a far-away voice was screaming, "You've sunk us! "

"Is it *us*?" gasped Harvey.

"No! A boat out yonder," cried Dan. "Keep ringing! We're going to lower a dory."

In half a minute, all the crew except Harvey, Penn, and the cook were out in dories, searching the sea. Part of a mast drifted past. Then an empty green dory banged against the side of the *We're Here*. It was followed by something in a blue jersey that had once been a whole man. At the sight of it, Penn, on deck, changed color and caught his breath.

Dan was the first to report back, fighting down hysteria as he did so. "It was the *Jennie Cushman*," he cried. "Cut clean in half and ground up as well. Dad's got the old man — the captain. He's all that's left. His son went down with the rest." Sobbing, he dropped his head on his arms and clutched the rail for support.

The Remains of the *Jennie Cushman*

CAPTAINS COURAGEOUS

By now, Disko and Manuel were dragging a protesting gray-haired man aboard.

"Why did you pick me up, Disko?" groaned the man. "Why did you bother?"

Disko put a comforting hand on the man's shoulder, but the stranger turned away, his eyes wild and his lips trembling.

Suddenly, Penn stepped forward and spoke in a wise, commanding voice — a voice that no one had ever heard from him before. "The Lord gave, and the Lord hath taken away. I was — I am a minister. Leave him to me."

The stranger roused himself and said bitterly, "If you're a minister, then pray my son back to me and my nine-thousand-dollar boat and my season's catch that was on board! It's your fault, Disko, that I'm alive. Better that I were dead than have to face my wife and tell her our boy is gone!"

"Jason Olley, there ain't nothing I can say to you," said Disko, knowing he was helpless to console the man. "Best lie down a bit."

Rescuing a Despairing Man

Penn put a hand on Captain Olley's arm. "Come below with me," he ordered.

Their eyes met, and Olley wavered. "All right, I'll go with you, whoever you are."

Penn led Olley into the cabin and slid the door shut. The crew could hear the two men talking, then Penn alone.

Uncle Salters whipped off his hat. "Penn praying. He's remembered! His eyes was wild as Jason Olley's. No doubt they were seeing that Johnstown flood."

The cabin door opened and Penn came out. Looking at the crew as if they were strange to him, he announced, "I prayed for this man's son. I prayed that he might be found alive and not like mine, drowned in front of me."

The man at whom the crew now stared was a stranger to them. Penn stood tall and straight with his shoulders back. He held his head proudly, unlike the shy Penn they knew. But the biggest change was his voice, which was confident and deep.

Penn Takes Charge of Olley.

The new Penn asked, "How long have I been mad?"

"Oh, now, Penn," protested Salters, "you wasn't mad, only a bit distracted."

"I saw my wife and children sink and a house followed. That is the last I remember. How long ago was that?" Penn asked.

Disko answered in a shaking voice, "That was about five years back."

"Then for five years someone has been taking care of me." He looked from one face to another. "Who has done so?"

Disko pointed to Uncle Salters.

"Ye didn't need no care," cried Salters, twisting his hands together. "Ye earned your keep, and ye was good company."

"You're a good man," pronounced Penn. "You're all good men. I see it in your faces."

"He don't know us," whispered Long Jack, more to himself than to Harvey, who was standing next to him. "All these trips as shipmates and he don't know us!"

Disko Explains About Uncle Salters to Penn.

The bell of a schooner sounded, and a voice came through the fog. "O Disko, have ye heard about the *Jennie Cushman?*"

Penn spun around and stared at the approaching schooner. "They have found his son! Get to your knees and thank the Lord! "

Disko went to the rail. "We got Jason on board," he called. Then his voice almost broke as he asked, "Was . . . was anyone else picked up?"

"Only one. We found him tangled in a pile of lumber. Cut him up some around the head, but it kept him afloat."

"Who is he?"

All heartbeats on the *We're Here* stopped for a moment.

"Young Olley," came the answer.

Penn raised his hands skyward in thankfulness.

The other schooner was the *Carrie Pitman,* whose captain was a distant relation of Jason Olley. She was headed back to Gloucester for

Kept Afloat on a Pile of Lumber

more bait, so plans were made to transfer the elderly captain to her, to be with his son.

Penn hurried to the cabin and woke Olley from a sleep of exhaustion and despair. The old man stumbled obediently after Penn, not yet knowing what awaited him on the *Carrie Pittman.* So he left without a word of thanks, for he still did not consider it a kindness that Disko had saved him.

As Tom Platt rowed Jason Olley to the other ship, Penn looked around triumphantly. He drew in a deep breath and said in a voice loud enough to carry the length of the *We're Here,* "Now you see how...how —" Suddenly, his voice faltered, and his erect body sank inward. The light faded from his overbright eyes; then, looking up shyly, he said in pitiful confusion, "Uncle Salters, do you think it's too early for a little game of checkers?"

Salters' mouth fell open in amazement, but he was quick to recover. "Just the thing, just the thing. I was going to suggest it myself. It

Penn's Mind Gives Way Again.

beats all, Penn, how you latch on to what a man is thinking."

Penn blushed at the compliment and meekly followed Uncle Salters into the cabin.

"Up anchor and hurry!" shouted Disko. "Let's leave these crazy waters!" And never was he more swiftly obeyed.

Once they were underway and out of the fog, the crew tried to explain to each other what had happened. Finally Disko's interpretation was accepted. "As Harvey pointed out, Penn got a shock seeing that crushed body drift by. It was like the Johnstown flood, all the water and the hurt people. Took him right back. So he remembered. Then ministering to Jason held him up a bit. But his mind was weak, and soon give way again. Like a boat, he slid back into the water. And he forgot."

The next day Salters added his conviction. "It's my belief that Penn prayed young Olley right out of the ocean."

And no one disagreed.

"Up Anchor and Hurry!"

Making Room for More Cod

CHAPTER 10

Caplin, Cod, and ... Whales

For the next three or four days, Disko worked all hands very hard until the fate of the *Jennie Cushman* began to fade from their minds. Penn remained the Penn they knew. When fog kept the crew shipbound, Disko ordered them into the hold to stack the ship's stores into smaller spaces to make more room for the salted cod.

The men were finishing this task one morning when Disko shouted down to them, "Hurry, boys! We're in town! The whole Banks fleet has come to meet the cod in this one place."

Harvey and Dan rushed up on deck. The sun was just clear of the horizon. Its low red light struck the sails of three fleets of anchored schooners, nearly a hundred of every possible make and build, bobbing up and down in the water as if they were courtseying to each other.

From every boat, dories were dropping away like bees from a crowded hive. The clamor of voices, the rattling of ropes and tackle, and the splash of oars carried for miles across the heaving water.

As the sun mounted, the dories gathered in clusters, separated, re-formed, and broke again, all heading in one direction.

"It *is* a town," cried Harvey. "Disko was right."

"I've seen smaller," said Disko. "There's about a thousand men here."

The *We're Here* skirted around the fleet to the north while Disko waved his hand to friend after friend. As the whole Banks fleet watched

A Town of Hundreds of Schooners

critically, Disko anchored.

"Just in time for the caplin," called a voice from the *Mary Chilton,* referring to a small silver fish much like a smelt.

"Is your salt still wet?" asked the *King Philip.*

"Hey, Tom Platt! Come over to supper tonight," invited the *Henry Clay.*

Questions flew back and forth among old friends, and since the Banks fleet were great gossipers, everyone soon knew about Harvey's rescue.

As the boys rowed to join the dories headed for the caplin, boat banging boat, Harvey became the object of many comments from the men they passed. Although these comments were in French and Portuguese and Gaelic, he could interpret from the tone of voice and the gestures and laughter that accompanied them that they were openly criticizing his rowing. And for the first time in his life, Harvey Cheyne felt shy.

Laughter over Harvey's Rowing

When they reached the fishing area, Dan handed Harvey a dip-net. "When I say *dip,* you dip. The caplin'll school any time now, and the cod'll follow them. We best be ready."

The sea around them clouded and darkened. Tiny silver fish fizzed up from the deep like freshly opened soda-water. After them came the cod, leaping like trout. And behind the cod, also heading for the caplin, were three or four whales.

Tom Platt, who was leading the little fleet of the *We're Here's* dories, had anchored them right in the middle of the six acres filled with their catch.

Harvey dipped furiously. Other dories headed for their area, the men swearing at their anchors and each other. In the tumult, Harvey was almost knocked overboard by the handle of Dan's net. As he regained his feet, he saw a broad gray back almost level with the water. Its head turned and stared at Harvey through a wicked little eye. The whale moved off, and

Caplin, Cod, and . . . Whales!

Harvey plunged his net in among the caplin again and again.

The caplin moved off and lines were put over the side. Harvey could see the glimmering cod below, swimming slowly in droves. The whack of the muckles was steady as cod after cod was hauled in. It was wonderful fishing.

The caplin schooled once more at twilight, and the mad clamor was repeated. At dusk, Harvey and Dan rowed back with the others to dress down by the light of kerosene lamps on the edge of the pen.

It was a huge pile of cod. One by one, the crew dropped off to sleep while they were dressing down. As Harvey nodded off, he again saw the whale's tiny, wicked eye looking at him, so close, so dangerous. It startled him awake. When he saw that he was safe on the *We're Here,* he gave a sigh of relief and sank into the sleep of exhaustion.

Asleep on Their Feet

A Funeral at Sea

CHAPTER 11

A Dead Man's Knife

One of the fleet of schooners assembled in the area was a Frenchman, the same boat that had traded tobacco to the *We're Here*. A fierce, roaring wave the night before had caught one of her crew, broken his back, and killed him.

The next morning, Harvey saw the ship moving into deep water for the funeral. Borrowing Disko's spyglass, Harvey watched an oblong bundle slide over the side, with no service accompanying it.

At anchor that night, a slow, hymn-like song came over the black water from the

Frenchman. Harvey and Dan listened without speaking, though Manuel hummed quietly along.

Harvey and Dan were fishing from the *Hattie S.* the next morning when another dory pulled past them.

"They're auctioning off his belongings," called the man. There was no need to ask whose belongings, for they saw a crowd of dories heading toward the Frenchman.

Dan looked over at Harvey. "Shall we go see what's there?" he asked. "It'll give us a chance to get warmed up too."

Harvey nodded, and they began to row. "Won't his family want his things?" he asked Dan.

Dan shrugged. "Tom Platt said there wasn't any family. Though, an auction ain't the usual way to do things."

The dead man's belongings were spread out on the deck for all to see, from his red knitted cap to his leather belt with a sheath and knife

"They're Auctioning Off His Belongings."

at the back. After examining the things, Dan bought the dead man's knife, which had a curious brass handle. Included in the price was the sheath and leather belt.

Back in the *Hattie S.*, they pushed off in a drizzle of rain, which made them shiver in their oilskin jackets. In a moment they were in the heart of a white fog, which dropped on them without warning. Though they could not see a boat's length in any direction, Harvey was not frightened. This was a fisherman's life. So they dropped their lines and found the cod biting well.

Dan drew out his new knife and examined the edge. "You notice how all his shipmates stepped back when I bid?" he asked.

"Yes," replied Harvey. "They let you get it cheap. Why was that?"

"They're superstitious about taking knives from a dead man."

"But an auction isn't *taking* anything," protested Harvey. "It's business."

Examining the Dead Man's Knife

"Their superstitions don't hold to that. And besides, the captain of the Frenchman told me this knife was used on the French coast last year."

Harvey's eyes opened wide. "Used? You mean used *on* somebody?"

"Killed him! Of course when I heard that, I was keener than ever to get it," said Dan.

"Think of that!" said Harvey. "Say, I'll give you a dollar for it when I get paid. No, I'll give you two dollars."

"Honest? You like it all that well?" said Dan, flushing. "Well, to tell you the truth, I kinda got it for you. I already have a knife and I saw you didn't have any, and so being dorymates and all, I . . . . Still, I didn't want to tell you until I knew what you thought of the knife. So take it and welcome, Harv." And he handed the knife and belt to Harvey.

Harvey just stared at the gift for a few moments, then protested weakly, "Oh, naw, Dan, you were the one bought it. I don't—"

Harvey Protests Dan's Gift.

"Take it," insisted Dan. "I want you to have it. Now that's an end to it."

Harvey struggled against taking the gift for a few more seconds, then accepted it eagerly. "Well, thanks, Dan, thanks a lot. I'll keep it as long as I live."

"That's good to hear," said Dan with a pleased smile. "Hey, it looks as if your line's hooked onto something."

Harvey fastened the belt around himself before turning to tug on his line. "It's fouled, I guess. It could be a strawberry-bottom."

Dan reached over and gave Harvey's line a tweak. "Sometimes a halibut'll act that way. Yank her once or twice and see if she gives."

Harvey yanked on the line and it seemed to give. Then Dan decided they'd better make certain what was hooked, so they hauled up together. Dan hooked each length of line around the boat's cleats to make it fast as the weight rose sluggishly.

"Here she comes! Haul!" shouted Dan, but

Yanking on the Line Together

his shout ended in a double shriek of horror. For out of the sea rose the body of the dead Frenchman, cast into the water two days before! The hook had caught him under the right armpit. Now he swayed, erect and horrible, his head and shoulders above the water. His arms were tied behind him. And — he had no face!

The boys clutched one another and cowered in a heap at the bottom of the dory. The faceless body continued to bob alongside, held on the shortened line.

"Oh, Harv! Quick, quick! Take the belt off! He's come for it," cried Dan.

Harvey fumbled with the buckle of the belt. "I don't want it!" groaned Harvey. He got the belt open and whispered to Dan, "The line's still holding him fast."

Together they looked at the head that had no face under its streaming hair. Dan slipped out his knife and cut Harvey's line. At the same time, Harvey flung the belt with the

A Faceless Man Surfaces!

sheathed knife far over the side. The body shot down at once, and Dan cautiously rose to his knees, his face white as the fog.

"I've seen a body hauled up on a trawl, and it didn't bother me none. But *he* come to us special," he said.

Harvey shook his head, still dazed. "I wish — I wish I hadn't taken the knife. Then he would have come on your line." Then he gave himself a mental shake. "But how could he come to us *special?* It was the tide."

"Tide?" scoffed Dan, his voice still shaky.

"Why, they sunk him six miles south of the fleet, and we're two miles beyond that. They told me he was weighted with a fathom and a half of chain-cable."

Harvey did not argue further. "Wonder what it was that made him kill that man up on the French coast?"

"Whatever it was, he must be needing that knife again and . . . what are you doing with the fish, Harv?"

Returning the Dead Man's Knife

"Heaving them overboard."

"Why? *We* won't be eating 'em."

"I don't care," said Harvey, throwing back fish after fish. "I had to look at his face while I was taking off the belt. You can keep your catch if you want. I've no use for mine."

Dan said nothing, but started throwing his fish over the side too.

When they had cleared the boat of cod, Dan said, "I wish this fog would lift. Things happen in a fog that you won't see in clear weather. One good thing, though, I'm glad he come the way he did instead of walking and searching us out in the night."

"Stop it, Dan!" cried Harvey. "Remember we're still on top of him. I wish we were back safe on the *We're Here.*"

"They'll be looking for us in a while. Hand me the tooter."

Harvey passed the dinnerhorn to Dan, who did not blow it but sat looking at it thoughtfully.

Throwing the Cod over the Side

"Go on, blow," urged Harvey. "I don't want to stay here all night."

"The question is, how might *he* take it," replied Dan, with a look and nod down at the sea. "A man from down the coast once told me that on his ship they didn't dare blow a horn to call in the dories. The skipper that had owned her once had drowned a boy when he tried to haul in his dory and was too drunk to do it right. So ever after when they'd blow a horn in the fog, that boy would row alongside with the rest, calling, 'Dory Dory!'"

"Dory! Dory!" a muffled voice cried through the fog.

Dan dropped the horn, and the boys cowered in the bottom of the dory. Then the call came again.

Harvey raised his head and said, "Hold on! That sounded like the cook."

Dan sat up and peered into the fog. "Sure it does. I don't know why I thought of that fool tale. It was a dumb thing to do." Then he sang

A Voice from the Fog

out, "It's me and Harvey! Over here."

They heard oars, but could see nothing until the cook rowed up alongside.

"What happened?" asked the cook. "You be beaten for giving us trouble. We all look for you."

"We'd welcome a beating," said Dan seriously, "just so's we're safe aboard again."

As the cook passed them a line, Dan told him what had happened. The cook listened in silence, then said, "Yes, I see it as the truth. He came for his knife."

The cook, with his second sight, rowed them unerringly to the *We're Here*. A warm glow of light from the cabin and the smell of delicious fried pork and hot bread greeted them. For Harvey and Dan it was heavenly to hear Disko and the others at the rail promising them a good beating for the worry and trouble they'd caused — because it meant that they were home at last.

But the cook had a plan of his own, and so

The Cook Rows Them Back.

before he latched the ropes to his dory, he recounted to Disko and the crew the most striking points of the boys' tale of the knife. Then he gave his opinion that Harvey was a mascot to destroy any possible bad luck.

Impressed, the crew took the boys aboard as heroes of a strange and wonderful tale, and even laughed at the superstition surrounding it. There was no beating, but, instead, respectful questions.

Later, though Penn and Salters scoffed, the cook put a lighted candle, a cake of flour and water, and a pinch of salt on a shingle and floated them onto the sea. It was meant to keep the Frenchman quiet in case he was still restless. Dan lit the candle because he had bought the belt. And the cook kept murmuring incantations as long as he could see the flame.

Thus, when Harvey went to bed, he didn't have the bad dreams he feared would haunt him thereafter.

Heroes of a Strange and Wonderful Tale!

Everyone Is Put To Work.

CHAPTER 12

Homeward Bound!

The *We're Here* was racing neck and neck against the *Parry Norman* to fill up first with a full load of cod. The struggle was so close that the fleet took sides and bet tobacco. Everyone fished or dressed down, and it became a regular matter to fall asleep at the pen with a half-cleaned cod and a knife in one's hands. Harvey was stationed in the hold to pass the salt, and the cook was taught to pitch the cod.

Luckily, a *Parry Norman* man sprained his ankle, and the *We're Here* gained the advantage. By this time, Harvey did not see how another fish could be crammed into the *We're*

Here, but Disko and Tom Platt stowed and stowed, and weighed the mass down with heavy boards and stones. Every night, Disko would announce "just one more day's work." The crew didn't know that all the salt was wet until Disko began hauling out the big mainsail at ten o'clock one morning.

Soon, dories from the rest of the fleet were coming alongside with letters for the *We're Here* to carry home. At last, the *We're Here* hoisted her flag, a right belonging to the first ship off the Banks. She up-anchored and began to move.

Disko, pretending he wished to accommodate folks who had not got their mail to him, sailed gracefully in and out among the schooners. In reality, this was his little triumphant procession — one he had been able to make for five years in a row.

Dan played his accordion while Tom Platt sang the song that was forbidden until all the salt was wet: "Hi! Yi! Yoho! Send your letters

Collecting the Mail for Home

'round! All our salt is wetted, and the anchor's off the ground."

The last letters were pitched on deck, wrapped around pieces of coal. Men from Gloucester shouted messages to their wives and owners. Then the *We're Here* headed west by south for home.

Harvey soon discovered how different it was to sail with heavy sails up from under light sail as they had been doing. Now, there was a bite and kick to the wheel. Alongside, the streaming line of bubbles made his eyes dizzy. Disko kept them busy fiddling with the sails to gain every bit of speed. In spare moments they pumped, for the packed fish dripped brine.

Since there was no fishing, Harvey had time to watch the splendid upheaval of a red sunrise or the wind herding clouds across the sky. He also had time to eat doughnuts and lie on the deck, with bare feet and arms, talking aimlessly to Dan.

Dan predicted, "Next Sunday, you'll be

Heading for Home

hiring someone to throw water on your bed-room windows ashore so you can get to sleep. Do you know what the best part of getting ashore is?"

Since his eyebrows were all white with dried spray, Harvey guessed, "A hot bath?"

"That's good, but a nightshirt's better," replied Dan. "Ma'll have a new one for me, all washed soft. You know, I think I'm beginning to smell the bayberries. I guess you'll stay with us until your folks can come for you?"

Harvey nodded happily.

They came into Gloucester Harbor in a wild summer storm. The lightning flickered off and on, and lit up the low circle of hills around the harbor, the fish-sheds, and the houses.

Because it was the middle of the night, Disko whispered his orders that led them to Wouverman's wharf. They skirted moored tugs, from which came the sound of snoring. Disko nosed the *We're Here* into a pocket of darkness where a lantern glimmered on either

Coming into Gloucester in a Storm

side. There, the night watchman wakened with a grunt and threw them a rope. They made fast to a long, silent wharf lined with large, empty, iron-roofed sheds.

The darkness and the silent procession of the *We're Here* toward home had built up a tension in Harvey unlike any he had ever known. He felt the land close around him once more, with all of its thousands of people asleep. He smelled the earth after rain, and heard the familiar noise of a switching-engine coughing in a freight yard. All these things made his heart beat fast and his throat dry up. Sitting down by the wheel, Harvey Cheyne sobbed as though his heart would break.

Just before dawn, a tall, smiling woman came along the wharf and dropped down into the boat. She was Dan's mother and had seen the *We're Here* by the lightning flashes. Kissing Dan once on the cheek, she didn't notice the sobbing Harvey until she had heard his story from Disko.

Dan's Mother Comes On Board.

Then, as dawn broke, she led them to Disko's house. Harvey suddenly felt like the loneliest boy in America, but he was relieved to see that neither Disko nor Dan seemed to think any the worse of him for crying.

As soon as the telegraph office opened, Harvey sent a wire to his parents. Later, he received one which he showed only to Dan.

Wouverman, the wharf owner, was not ready to accept Disko's prices. But since Disko was sure that the *We're Here* was at least a week ahead of any other fishing boat, he held to his prices, knowing he could afford to wait a few days until they were accepted.

The crew enjoyed their leisure, but everything was not peaceful. Dan went about with his freckled nose in the air and, full of mystery, treated everybody, including his family, in a superior manner.

Finally, Disko could tolerate it no longer. "I'm of the opinion that a beating might be overdue," he told Dan. "You've been a heap too

Harvey Sends a Wire to His Parents.

fresh since we came ashore."

Backing away from his father toward the front door of the house, Dan called out, "You're welcome to your own opinion, just as I'm welcome to mine. And what's more, I'm not one to make a msisjudgment after I been told different. So we'll just wait and see who is mistaken."

Disko shook his head and sighed. "You're getting as crazy as poor Harv. You two go around giggling and kicking and pinching each other till there's no peace in the house."

After this exchange, Dan and Harvey took the trolley to East Gloucester, where they tramped through the bayberry bushes to the lighthouse, laughing explosively from time to time. One would set the other off until they had to lie on the big red boulders, their sides aching from laughing.

And inside Harvey's pocket, the telegram from his father heated up like a shell ready to burst.

Laughing Over Their Shared Secret!

Grief for a Dead Son

CHAPTER 13

News of a Miracle

At the terrible news of Harvey's disappearance from the liner, his father had dropped everything and rushed east to meet his wife. He almost did not recognize her. The handsome, beautifully-dressed, charming woman that had been Constance Cheyne had disappeared. In her place was a bedridden madwoman. Cheyne could not allow himself time to grieve over his son, for all his energies had to go toward saving his wife.

Money poured out. A brilliant young doctor was persuaded — at a price — to give up all his patients except one, Mrs. Cheyne. He directed a stream of nurses, maids, and companions to spoon-feed her all her meals and to wake her from her nightmares. Gradually, the doctor had guided her back from madness until now she was a despairing invalid, but alive and in her right mind.

She asked only to have someone beside her at all times to whom she could talk about Harvey. The companions, nurses, and doctors listened sympathetically and pretended interest in stories about the boy's short life, which they heard over and over. Mrs. Cheyne wanted comfort, though she did not ask for hope. She knew there could be no hope, but she wanted to be reassured that drowning did not hurt.

After that, the doctor gave the companions another order: Mrs. Cheyne must be watched at all times so that she wouldn't experiment with drowning herself.

Now, Mrs. Cheyne, the doctor, and all the attendants occupied one entire wing of the Cheyne mansion in San Diego. Another wing

Mrs. Cheyne Talked About Harvey.

was used by Mr. Cheyne as his business offices. He had installed a private telegraph line and an operator, along with his many assistants and his male secretary. With his wife safe in professional hands, he could turn back to business: to the rate war between his railroad and three other Western ones, to legislation adverse to himself that the state of California was considering, and to any number of strikes at his lumber camps. But he had no heart for any of these matters and found himself constantly thinking, "What's the use?"

Though preoccupied with making money, he had always expected to have Harvey succeed him. It was a vague dream he had had that Harvey would graduate from college and, at that golden moment, father and son would become close friends and partners, and he would guide Harvey into becoming a captain of industry like himself.

He was glancing at his mail while his

Mr. Cheyne's Dream for Harvey

secretary, Milsom, stood by for replies one Saturday morning, when he heard the telegraph operator in the next room give a yelp. He raised his eyebrows inquiringly, and his secretary hurried to find out what bad news about railroad rates had come over the wire. The operator had never before given way to amazement, so Milsom expected the worst. He returned in a moment with a telegram, his face very white.

"Well, read it to me," Cheyne ordered.

In a shaking voice Milsom read: *"Picked up by fishing schooner We're Here, having fallen off boat STOP great times on Banks fishing STOP all well STOP waiting Gloucester Mass care Disko Troop for money or orders STOP wire what shall do STOP how is mama STOP Harvey N. Cheyne, Jr."*

Harvey N. Cheyne, Sr., reached out a trembling hand for the telegram and reread it. Then, breathing heavily, he let his head fall forward onto his desk. Frightened, Milsom ran

Reaching Out a Trembling Hand

into the other wing to summon the doctor.

The doctor found Cheyne up and pacing around his office like a caged animal. "What do you think?" he cried. "Is it possible?"

Milsom had told the news to the doctor, who replied, "Why not? There's no motive for a trick or fraud without the culprit getting caught. No, I'm certain it's the boy."

One of Mrs. Cheyne's maids ran into the room. "Madam says you must come to her at once. She fears you are ill."

Grabbing the telegram from his desk, the master of thirty million dollars hurried to his wife. She was standing at the head of staircase, her face strained with anxiety. "What is it? What has happened?" she cried.

Cheyne put his arm around her shoulders and led her back into her bedroom, motioning the two companions out.

Taking his wife into his arms, Harvey Cheyne said quietly, "Harvey's alive. He was picked up by a fishing schooner."

Hurrying to His Wife

Mrs. Cheyne's eyes widened, a little moan escaped her, and then she gave a scream of joy. "Where is he? We must go to him!"

"Massachusetts, Gloucester. We'll leave at once in the *Constance,*" replied Cheyne, referring to one of his private railroad cars.

By now Mrs. Cheyne was crying with happiness, and he hugged her, tears streaming down his own face as well.

A whirlwind of activity stirred the mansion. Milsom and the telegraph operator sent numerous telegrams to the railroad to route the *Constance* straight through from San Diego to Gloucester without stopping. Division superintendents were ordered to accompany this special train over their territory. The *Constance* was to take precedence over one hundred twenty-seven other trains, and all their schedules had to be rearranged. Two and a half minutes would be allowed for changing engines, three for watering, and two for coaling. Sixteen locomotives would

Tears of Joy!

be needed. When the timing was worked out, Harvey was wired of the hour to meet his parents at the Boston railroad station.

Mrs. Cheyne was instantly transformed into a thinner version of her former self, high on energy and pleased with the world.

The Cheynes left in an hour's time to board the *Constance*. Mr. Cheyne demanded a speed of forty miles an hour, and his engineers delivered it, knowing the purpose of their mission. Their total running time was three days, fifteen and a half hours — a record time!

As the *Constance* pulled into the station at Boston, the Cheynes were ready to descend as soon as the steps of the train were let down. Mr. Cheyne went first, then helped his wife down. As they looked up, they saw Harvey walking — then running — toward them.

Racing Toward Boston in Record Time!

Reunion!

CHAPTER 14

Two Captains Meet

The reunion between Harvey and his parents provided mixed emotions. Mrs. Cheyne was hysterically happy. Harvey was delighted to see his parents, but mostly eager to tell them his adventures and the merits of the *We're Here* and her crew. Mr. Cheyne was filled with wonder that this sturdy, straight-backed boy in a blue jersey and rubber boots could be his son. He remembered a sour-faced youth with a haughty manner, who frequently had tantrums when denied his slightest wish in hotels or restaurants. Though he had not seen much of his son, he recalled the veiled contempt and impatience with which Harvey used to address him. Now he noted a respectful tone and a clear, steady gaze that met his own unflinchingly.

At a Boston hotel, Mr. Cheyne ordered a splendid meal sent to a private dining room. While they ate, Mrs. Cheyne didn't take her eyes off Harvey and frequently reached over to touch his hand. Even after Harvey had repeated his story twice, she murmured, "What kind of man can this Troop person be that he wouldn't take you home? Papa would have made it up to him ten times over."

"Disko Troop is the best man that ever walked a deck," replied Harvey. "But he thought I was crazy. Finally, he had to wallop me to clear my head."

Mrs. Cheyne shuddered. "My poor darling!"

"No," said Harvey with a laugh, "he was right. After that, I saw the light."

His father laughed with him and thought, "This is going to be a boy to be proud of, a boy

Harvey Describes His Life at Sea.

after my own hungry heart!"

Harvey went on. "And he took me on for ten and a half a month, though I was raw then. But I learned to steer and handle a dory, and I know my ropes and how to pitch fish and a heap of things. It takes a lot of work to earn ten and a half a month."

"I began with eight and a half, son," said Mr. Cheyne. "I'll tell you about it sometime."

Harvey looked at him eagerly. "I'd like that, sir. Disko says there's nothing so interesting as how the next man earns his bread."

Finally, worn out after the hours of excitement, the Cheyne family went to bed early on the *Constance*. During the night, the private train made the run to Gloucester, for Harvey's work was not yet finished. And besides, Harvey wanted to show Disko that he wasn't crazy after all.

Harvey had been assigned the job of tally-man for the *We're Here,* so he left early the next morning for the wharves. His father had

Harvey Still Has a Job To Do.

suggested hiring a substitute, but Harvey was indignant at the idea of passing his responsibility on to another.

Mr. and Mrs. Cheyne appeared at Wouverman's wharf on a bright, sunny morning a few hours after Harvey. They watched loaded baskets of fish being swung from the *We're Here* to a scale where each was weighed. Harvey stood at the scale with his talley-sheets, checking the weigher's figures.

When the last basket had been swung down, Disko called out, "Total, Harv?"

"Eight sixty-five. Three thousand six hundred and seventy-six dollars *and* a quarter," Harvey called back.

After Harvey was sent to Wouverman's office with his total, the Cheynes moved closer. For the first time, Harvey Cheyne, Sr., a captain of industry, spoke to Disko Troop, a captain of a fishing schooner. "Is that boy worth his keep?" he asked.

"He's a good boy and catches on quick,"

Watching Their Son at Work

Disko replied courteously to the strangers. "He was some mixed-up in his head when we found him, but he's clear now."

"I'm glad to hear it," said Cheyne. "He is our son, Mr. Troop. May we come on board?"

Disko Troop nodded silently as Harvey Cheyne, Sr., took his hand and shook it.

As he led them on board the *We're Here,* Disko looked at the elegantly dressed couple beside him and at the diamonds that Mrs. Cheyne wore. His mouth dropped open and he was speechless. The rest of the crew, except Dan, were rigid with astonishment. For a few moments, nothing could be heard except some muffled giggles coming from Dan.

When they reached the deck, Disko finally managed to speak. "I was — I am mistook in my judgment," he began. "I didn't believe the boy when he talked about money, especially when he said he had lost a hundred and thirty dollars."

Mrs. Cheyne said, "A steward found it by

Two Captains Meet.

the flagpole after he disappeared."

Tom Platt, who had followed the Cheynes, along with the rest of the crew, spoke up. "Did he ever have a coach with four ponies?"

"Oh, yes," she replied, "it was fun."

"And do you have two private railroad cars?" asked Dan.

Mr. Cheyne nodded, smiling. "In fact, one of them is in a siding near the wharf, and we hope you'll all do us the honor of having lunch on her. But first, Mr. Troop, my wife and I would like to be introduced to your fine crew. We know all your names and all about every last one of you, but we want to thank each man personally."

In a daze, Disko presented each man. Mrs. Cheyne gave no thought to her fancy dress and white gloves as she shook each man's grimy hand with such gratitude that they felt shy. When she came to Manuel, she hugged him, even though she got fish scales all over the feathers on her hat as she did so.

Manuel Gets a Hug of Gratitude.

By now, Harvey had returned to the *We're Here* and was thoroughly enjoying the amazement of every man in the crew.

Disko motioned him over. "I want to apologize, Harvey, as you once apologized to me. I was mistook in my judgment. So don't rub it in anymore."

Harvey laughed, and Dan muttered under his breath, "No, *I'll* take care of doing that!"

Mr. Cheyne said, "Constance, why don't you take everyone to the railroad car for that lunch we invited them to. Mr. Troop and I will be along later after we talk in his cabin."

The two captains sat down, smoking Mr. Cheyne's imported cigars with enjoyment. Mr. Cheyne knew that Disko was a man to whom he could not offer money. He also knew that all the money he had could not repay Disko for all that he had done. So he said, "What plans do you have for Dan's future?"

"He'll have the *We're Here* when I'm gone. The sea's in his blood, like in mine."

Disko Apologizes to Harvey.

"I can give him all the sea he wants till he's a skipper," said Mr. Cheyne. "I own a line of iron-built tea-clippers that run from San Francisco to Japan."

"Harv told of railroads and ponies, but never of clippers," said Disko in awe. "I know a Gloucester man on a tea-boat, Phil Airheart. His sister's our neighbor, and she shows us his letters."

Cheyne nodded. "Airheart is a skipper on my line. I own the 'Blue M' freighters. What would you say to Dan signing on? We'll try to make a mate of him."

Disko thought it over. "Airheart writes they're mighty fine ships. And my wife would be pleased if Dan could ship out on something more stable than a schooner and her dories. But you're taking a risk with a raw boy—"

"I know a man who did just that — and more — for me," said Mr. Cheyne quietly.

Disko brushed aside the comment with his hand. "That was different. Now, Dan knows a

"That Was Different."

lot, even though a clipper's quite different from a fishing boat. But I got to tell you he's weak in navigation. Harvey's got twice the head that Dan has for figures. You saw how he tallied up today."

"Airheart will attend to that. You and he work on improving Dan's head for figures over the winter, and I'll send for the boy in the early spring. I know the Pacific's a long way off, but any time you and your wife want to see him, I'll pay all your expenses there and back."

Just then, Dan poked his head into the cabin. "Say, Dad, Mrs. Cheyne says food's about ready. Will you be through soon?"

"Come here, son," called Disko. Then he told him of Cheyne's offer. "It's for you to decide. This is not a chance that comes every day."

Dan's eyes lit up as he listened. When his father had finished, Dan turned to Mr. Cheyne and stammered, "Oh, gosh, I ... I ... a tea-clipper ... Japan ... I always wanted .... "

Disko Calls Dan In.

Mr. Cheyne smiled. "I take it you mean yes?"

"Oh, yes, sir! Thank you a thousand times. Think of it — a seventeen-hundred-and-eighty ton clipper!" His eyes glazed over as he saw himself in command on a broad deck, sailing into faraway harbors, bringing his ship home in record time. Mr. Cheyne had explained that he gave a bonus for a fast run, since tea did not improve by being at sea.

With Dan's future settled, they joined the others on the *Constance*. The crew was still awed by the private car with its silver doorknobs and railings, its tables inlaid with rare woods, its velvet hangings, and Oriental carpets. The lunch table was laid with silver dishes, a linen cloth, and delicate glassware.

Mrs. Cheyne expected that the fishermen would be unaccustomed to such grandeur and snap the stems of the crystal glasses and upset the silver gravy boat, but she didn't care. These men had saved Harvey, had made

Dan Is Overjoyed!

a man of him. Nothing was too good for them!

To her surprise, they ate and handled the utensils with precision and delicacy. She didn't know that men who eat in cramped quarters in howling gales develop neat manners with a sureness of touch. Nor did they remain ill at ease. Once at the table, it was their familiar group with much laughter, especially over Wouverman's unhappiness at having to accept Disko's high prices for their catch.

Mr. Cheyne's expertise in finance was much admired as he analyzed the fishing business and its marketing problems. Another surprise to Mrs. Cheyne was how Harvey fit in with the group. She saw that he now had an identity she had not bought for him: He was a member of the crew of the *We're Here*.

After lunch, Mrs. Cheyne took Manuel aside. He had instantly become her favorite for his part in Harvey's rescue. "My husband and I want to reward you," she said, but

Lunch in a Private Railroad Car

Manuel refused the huge sum of money she suggested. She insisted.

"No, why should I take money?" asked Manuel, shaking his curly head. "I have my food, I have my smokes, I have a little wine. What more do I need?"

Mrs. Cheyne was not used to being refused and kept talking to him. Finally, Manuel said, "All right, I take some money. I have girl-friend here in Gloucester. Very pretty. I take five dollars to buy her a scarf, most beautiful scarf she ever see."

The argument was settled by the Cheynes' giving thousands of dollars to Manuel's church in his name — and five dollars to him for the scarf. As a result, blessings from the church were showered on Manuel and prayers were offered for his continued safety at sea.

After staying on for several weeks to get to know Gloucester and its people, the Cheynes finally left, leaving behind them a legend that

Manuel Refuses a Reward.

the town would never forget. With them left the cook of the *We're Here*. He had seen another vision, which told him his destiny lay with Harvey. He did not care what pay, if any, was given him, or even where he slept. Disko and the others tried to persuade him to ship out with them again, for cooks of his high caliber were not easily found.

All the cook would say was, "I go with Harvey. I have seen it in my dreams."

And since Mr. Cheyne thought one volunteer was worth five hired men, the cook came with them.

Leaving Gloucester...

Having a Son for the First Time

CHAPTER 15

The Prophecy Comes True

Having Harvey back affected the Cheynes in different ways. For Mrs. Cheyne, she had her son back in the flesh, but she had lost him in spirit. He was no longer the boy she used to know and dote on.

For Mr. Cheyne, it was like having a son for the first time. The old Harvey had been a spoiled stranger, but the new one became an admiring confidant to his father. Their closeness was cemented on the day that Mr. Cheyne told Harvey the story of his life, which he had never revealed to anyone before.

It began with an orphaned boy in Texas, uneducated and inexperienced, taking on every kind of job. It ended with willpower and natural intelligence triumphant and providing millions of dollars.

But Mr. Cheyne advised education first. "I could have avoided many a mistake and come along a lot faster if I had known the kind of thing you can get only from books, Harvey."

They talked at length and Harvey finally saw his father's point. A pact was made by them. Harvey was to finish college and then come into one of the Cheyne businesses.

"Can I choose which one now?" asked Harvey.

His father laughed and said, "Of course, but I expect you'll change your mind a dozen times before you graduate."

"No, Dad, I won't. I want to be in charge of your tea-clippers. And every summer I want to study their progress and learn all there is to know about running them."

Father and son shook hands on the deal.

A Pact Is Made.

Thus, three years later two young men met in front of the Cheynes' California mansion. Both were on horseback and had come from different directions.

"Hello, Harvey," said Dan Troop, dismounting and hurrying toward his friend.

"Hello, Dan," said Harvey Cheyne, pumping his friend's hand joyously. "I heard the great news — you're to be second mate next trip."

"That's right. And you, Harvey? Are you coming into the business soon?" asked Dan.

"Next fall for good," said Harvey.

A black man came out of the mansion and took charge of the young men's horses. It was the *We're Here's* cook, now the Cheynes' cook and Harvey's attendant and friend. The man nodded to Dan and said, "You see, it is as I predicted. He is master and you are his man."

The two young men nodded and smiled.

The prophecy, made many years before on the *We're Here,* had at last come true.

The Cook's Prophecy Has Come True.